# Troll's Issue

CHAPTERS OF TROLL'S ISSUE



Book by Tal Gryphonwall

ISBN 978-061524500-3
Artwork by JDKO

## Ch. 1 The Traveler

Edgar looked up the hill. The wind blew against the marsh grass flattening and raising it in long waves that rose and dipped below the road running alongside the hills. Storm clouds rumbled overhead. The farther up the hill Edgar crawled through the mud the more the black twisted trees reached for the darkened sky. Up over the hill down the other side into the village before nightfall, he wanted nothing more than this, but the shortcut he had taken was proving to be harder to travel than the road. He had thought to avoid the gigantic curve it made around the hill of Maekmorth, but the hill was harder to climb than he expected. Mud clung to his hands. Edgar slipped and slid trying to make his way up the steep hill by clawing at the grass and anything else that grew there. Lightning cracked the earth several miles away on the open fields below. Edgar flinched hearing the rumble of thunder behind him but he did not let go of the long grasses clutched between his fingers. He was almost up to where the ground leveled out and he would be able to walk upright, the way a man should walk.

Maekmorth, the hill was named Maekmorth. The name rolled around in Edgar's mind. He was trying to remember where he had heard that word before and why it nagged at the back of his mind thrusting upon him a sense of dread. Maekmorth, the name had no meaning in the human language he was quite sure, but then he did not know any other languages so why should it matter?

Edgar struggled up the hill rising from his knees to stand on the barren hump leading up to the top of the hill. There he finally saw the shapes farther up among the trees. They were not the stunted trees they appeared to be from the road. Edgar nearly lost his balance stumbling backward in his hurry to go back to the road he had left below. He remembered why the name Maekmorth was important. Maekmorth meant "Troll" in some foreign language.

Edgar did not remember what language. He did not care what language the word Maekmorth came from but he did care about the huge brown hairy shapes that were charging after him from the ridge of the hill now that he had been spotted. Half sliding, half running, he leapt down the hill fearing what might happen to him should he not make it to the road in time. He saw the road in hurried glimpses dividing his vision between the ground he covered in front of his feet and the road he was headed for at full speed. There was a traveler on that road but who the traveler was he could not see through the sweat that dripped from his brow. The salt water stung his eyes but he dared not take the time to swipe it away, not when his own hands were covered in mud. He did not want to be fleeing blind and mud was more difficult to see through than sweat. His feet struck a patch of slick grass and his body went down with a thump. Lucky for him the ground was so wet from this afternoons rains that his body kept sliding downward off the hill. Edgar let out a sound of sheer surprise but he would not have been so alarmed had he realized that he was sliding faster than he had been able to run. The huge beings above paused watching the human slip off the hill and tumble onto the road.

Edgar saw them, their depthless black eyes, staring down at him from between the wrinkles of their horrid leathery flesh. He cried out at the sight and grasped the traveler's legs, looking up into his face for the first time.

"Trolls!" he stared up into the darkness of the face beneath the cowl of the gray, fur cloak. "Help! Trolls!"

"Trolls?" questioned the traveler in a remarkably smooth voice.

Edgar did not have any more breath to reply. Panting heavily he simply pointed upward back towards the hill. The stranger threw back the cowl of his fur cloak and looked where the man directed him. Then he laughed. Edgar shivered. There was something terrible in that laugh that he could not comprehend.

"The Maekmorth?"

Edgar stared at the stranger realizing for the first time that he was not human. Silver eyes gleamed down at him narrowly. The stranger was taller than him making Edgar think he was slender, yet he was not. Muscles built over many years lined the stranger's arms. Edgar could feel the force of them when the stranger pulled him up and looked into his face. The silver eyes widened slightly. Edgar's own eyes watered from their brightness. He tried to focus on the stranger's thin nose, but the silver eyes that had narrowed back to slits drew his attention. He tried focusing past them to the sharp tipped ears on either side of the stranger's thin face that held back the long locks of muddy hair, but the silver light drew his focus in the way nothing else could. The stranger grinned revealing two teeth on either side among the rest of the white rows that were very sharp.

"You fear the Maekmorth," the stranger lifted him an inch higher, then threw him back down onto the muddy roadside. "Then fear me."

Edgar's head was flung back when he hit the mud splattering more of it onto the marshgrass nearest but his eyes were free of the stranger's gaze. He glanced back up towards the Maekmorth. The Trolls above showed their larger sharper teeth, grinning down at him until the biggest, shouted a guttural word Edgar did not understand, jumped onto the hillside, (landing on his rear), and slid down it faster than Edgar ever could have. The others followed their leader down. Edgar's head jerked back around towards the stranger, his only chance of survival.

"Help!" was all he could stutter.

"Sih Rih!" roared the biggest Troll on his way down the hillside of Maekmorth.

"Sih Rih?" The stranger shouted in reply leaping forward, grasping Edgar, and pulling him out of the mud.

Edgar clung to the stranger when the huge Trolls thumped onto the road, in the spot where Edgar had been sprawled, bringing with them most of the plants that had been in their way on the fast ride down. His nose was nearly touching the stranger's. He did not have much hope that the stranger could help him, but he needed someone to give him some sign of humanity in this horrid nightmare that he understood was no nightmare. The stranger had a weapon. He saw the hilt of it angling out over the stranger's left shoulder, but even with the blade between them, what could the two of them do against six Trolls?

"You are not a Troll! Help me!" Edgar's own gray eyes stung from having to look into the brightness of the stranger's eyes for too long, but this time he would not look away.

"Korrrr goth Mikroth Sih Rih," the large Troll spoke rising to its feet.

The stranger looked past Edgar towards the biggest Troll. Edgar glanced back once then decided it would be better to keep his gaze fixed on the stranger, for sanity's sake. The stranger was beautiful in an odd way but those other things were ugly. Horridly ugly!

"What did it say?" Edgar gasped. "What does 'Si Ri' mean?"

The stranger looked at him coldly. "Sih Rih means "save the meat."

Edgar's jaw dropped open in the same second that it took for a large gnarled hand to grab his skull. The large crooked fingers drew Edgar's body back into the embrace of hairy arms bulging with muscle.

"What are you?" shouted Edgar trying to struggle in the huge Troll's grasp. "To let a man die in front of your eyes and just watch?"

The sound of the human's ribs cracking did not make the stranger redirect his cold hard stare. The big Troll made a thundering noise expelling vile breath into the air. The other Trolls made the same noise. Edgar's eardrums throbbed with sheer pain.

"Misborn," the stranger replied under his breath. "Maekmorth."

The stranger said this too quietly to be heard, but it did not matter. Edqar would not have heard him anyway. The big Troll twisted the humans neck and Edgar's vision went black with a snap.

"Ev Vrin, Sih Rih!" the big Troll shouted holding the human's corpse.

Ev Vrin nodded slowly. He had done something to Crogar's approval for once, so why did it trouble him in the head? Ev Vrin shook it. There was not much meat on it but for some reason this kill pleased Crogar, but it did not please Ev. He had been training for this for a long time. Learning the sounds of the humans, studying the ways they fought by questioning all the elders of the clan of Kaed. Few of the Maekmorth bothered learning the human sounds but Jhahgror had kept, (before the time of Ev's birth), a human pet she had been very fond of and she had taken the time to learn what its sounds meant. Jhahgror had been happy to teach them to Ev. She had insisted it was so small a thing to do for one of the sons of the Great Chief Grael. Ev smiled grimly at that memory. Not that he was much of a son. The thought plagued him on his trudge back up the hill of Maekmorth after Crogar. Ev Vrin meant "frail one" in the tongue of the Maekmorth and he was frail compared to their brawny furthick hides. Crogar thumped him on the back.

The Troll's pleasantries would have sent Ev sprawling in the mud had he not been prepared. Regaining his balance again. Ev tried not to let the pain show in his movement. The slap had no doubt brought the color to his skin, but that would fade Ev reflected darkly, recalling years of torment in his youth when his siblings had discovered how pretty his skin looked when they pounded it hard enough. Blood had flowed then but every break of his skin had sealed over before the next could be made. His incredibly fast recovery had not dimmed the pain. He had made sounds similar to the flying Kiew's cries and the Rugar howls then. The sounds had delighted his siblings. He had learned not to do this. Growling was the proper noise, he had learned. His throat was malformed and it could not make the proper sounds of the Maekmorth tongue. He did his best but his throat was too weak. "Weak one" his siblings had called him. Frail one was what his own mother had named him. Ev shook his head again wondering why he always thought in the sounds of the humans. The sounds came easier to his throat than Maekmorth, the language of the Trolls. "Troll"...the human word for Maekmorth sounded so simple and it did not take so much work from the back of the throat to say.

*"You are not a Troll!"* Ev flinched remembering that the human had insulted him by accusing him of not being Maekmorth.

Not a Troll. Ev stared past the twisted trees. The Maekmorth came to a halt and Crogar ordered the fire to be lit. Ev stooped down taking out his flint and steel for the task. The pile of wood, including marsh grass and Maekmorth dung they had been gathered was more than enough. Mogrim sat beside it demanding to hear what had caused the delay, fingering the corpse thrust in front of her with a sharp smile. Ev remained silent, lighting the fire and listening to Crogar tell how he had made his great kill of the human warrior. Somehow Ev doubted the human had been a warrior. The human had not fought them with the sharp blade in its belt. Ev recalled that the human had not even thought to draw the small blade. Ev placed a hand over longest of the wicked blades he always carried and thought over the differences in what Crogar said and what he himself had witnessed. What he had seen was a scared creature, far more terrified than the mountain goats or the lone soft sheep that lost their way in the mountains and become dinner. There had been a time when he had tried to learn their sounds too, but their sounds were not the same. Maekmorth made more sense. The sounds the humans made worked the way Maekmorth did and he was impressed with his success of speaking with the human. He had wanted to make more sounds with it before they killed it.

Crogar ended his speech with an enormous grunt. Mogrim lifted the arm of the human, took a bite, then spat it out. The chunk of flesh sizzled in the fire.

"Mighty struggle, huh?" the thick hairs over her left eye rose. "From a thing that does not have enough meat on it to chew!"

Mogrim thrust the corpse aside in disgust. Crogar reached over, ripped the thing's head off, and presented it to Ev. Ev accepted the offering. Grasping the head by the hair, he stood, gave them all a sharp grin and walked away from the firelight. He would hang the head in the branches of the leafless tree signifying that he was not hungry and he would eat it tomorrow. He stared at the disfigured shape of the human's head when he hung it from the barren branches by its hair and felt his guts roll round. Mogrim had always insisted he had a small stomach. He did not eat enough. That was the reason he was so small and hairless. Ev's grim smile chiseled its way farther along his cheek. He had always understood that he was born disfigured and nothing would change that, but Mogrim was right. He did have a smaller stomach than the rest. It made things harder to digest.

Staring at the head he did not think he could eat it. The human's nose was not knobby. Not in the way of proper Maekmorth noses. Ev reached up to touch it. The nose was smooth in the same way of his own nose. A shiver leaped through Ev's body. The swift glance over his shoulder reassured him the other Trolls had not seen it. Ev let his eyelids fall. They leaked rain. Troll eyes did not leak rain. Ev grimaced. "Frail one" was his true name. More rain leaked from beneath his shut eyelids. The face of the human was there in his mind. He could not shake it out of his head. Inside he understood the frail face would be in his mind forever.

Ev Vrin had to be careful. The weakness of his hairless body had nearly caused his death many times. He had lost count after ten, most Trolls did not count higher than eight, but due to his extra fingers he had learned to count higher. Jhahgror had taught him in the manner of the humans. Ev left the head, suddenly walking swiftly back to the fire. Taking up the corpse he peered at it. Qwor had already eaten the left hand but the right was still there. He had to shove Qwor out of the way but he had never liked Qwor anyway. Qwor growled but he stopped when Ev drew his blade. Ev's growl was small compared to Qwor's but Qwor went back to eating. Ev had the reputation of wicked quick beheadings and Qwor had a certain fondness for his head. Ev's fierce smile faded when he looked down at the human's hand. He counted the fingers carefully. There were five on this hand. He dared not look at his own but he moved his fingers one by one counting them silently in his mind again to make certain there were ten. When he was finished, and he had sheathed his blade, he offered the hand to Mogrim. Kwat gave him a sharp wink from across the fire. They would think he was interested in her but he would prefer that to letting them discover his true interest in the corpse. Mogrim burped and spit out something she had found inedible from the human's remains. She held it out to him. Ev accepted the offering giving her a fierce grin before examining it in the firelight. Beneath the slime of the Mogrim's saliva it was round and hard. There were deep scratches on it Ev discovered. Scratches similar to the stone he wore around his own neck. The stone his mother insisted he was born with in the cave of births. The difference was that his stone was pierced clear through at the top. He had run a shaving of hide through it and tied it around his neck. The stone was there now against his hairless chest. Fear gripped him there. No wonder Jhahgror had taken an interest in him. This human looked more like him than the Trolls, and the stone.... Ev gripped it tightly in his hands. The stone was not a gem from deep beneath the earth that the Maekmorth would have treasured. The stone was plain and scraped in a manner that made it flawed in the minds of the Maekmorth in the same way that they saw he was flawed.

Ev stood a second time and walked away from the fire. Mogrim looked up but Ev growled letting her know he did not want to be followed. When a male wanted to leave the fire he did not need to give a reason. Ev moved farther up the hill named for the Maekmorth. He did not stop until he stood at its top. The storm clouds rumbled overhead and the air was ripe with the threat of rain. Not that it mattered any to the Maekmorth. The fire might go out but they did not need it since Mogrim had refused to cook their scrawny kill. The Maekmorth could see in the dark. Behind Ev lay the marsh but he did not need to turn his keen night vision back towards it to know it was there. Ev gazed down on the wind rushing through the long grass far to the north. It made him wonder whether humans, too, could see so far in the dark. Maybe they could and if they could what if...

The ears were round. He remembered staring at them when the human had clutched at his legs. Round, not pointed like the Maekmorth, and the human's teeth had not been sharp. Ev had been fascinated with the way the human had spoken and those smooth block shaped teeth. His own teeth were not sharp. He had been laughed at for their dullness. Jhahgror had shown him a way to sharpen them and it had been a source of pride that he now had two sharp teeth. Mogrim had smiled and told him it was her secret recipe for goat that had made them sharp. She had been so proud that he was finally growing into a proper Troll. Ev wiped the rain from his eyes. He understood the taunts now. He understood why old Traws had called him "Human Meat." Why had the Maekmorth not eaten him the same way they had eaten the human? This puzzled him greatly. They had killed other misborn but not Ev. Ev fingered the tip of his right ear. Maekmorth had sharp ears. Humans had smooth skin and watery eyes. Their eyes were not solid black. Ev opened his silver eyes and stood. Casting a glance back at the other Trolls he did not see any of them moving more than to relieve an irritating itch. Ev swung around and his stride took him down the hill past the Maekmorth. None awoke at his passing. Among the names he had been taunted with when he was younger was "light foot."

Troll stomping was beyond his thin limbs. Yesterday he would have tried to stomp hard enough to make them acknowledge his passing but this night he was glad he was light of foot. Ev walked down the hill with their snores booming out into the air behind him. Perhaps humans were not his people, but he no longer believed the Maekmorth were either. Thunder rumbled in the wake of the lightning that sizzled on the hilltop Ev had left. This was not a good time to leave but he needed to find a human and talk to it longer then it took to kill it. Ev slid down the last stretch of Maekmorth hill setting his right foot onto the road.

## Ch. 2 Being Human

Ev watched the human shapes walk into the town below him and mingle with the rest going about their daily errands; errands that made very little sense to Ev. They walked among the pointed caves they had made from wood making sounds to one another, carrying things, and sometimes making offerings. Not all the offerings were accepted and some humans refused to make an offering in return. Ev growled low beneath his breath thinking he would have to bring something back from the humans in return for Crogar's offering, assuming Crogar had not taken it back by now, and eaten it. Ev's silver eyes narrowed. He would offer it to Mogrim should the head still be there when he came back, that was "if" he chose to return. Crouched low behind a couple of bushes on the hillside he hid his presence from those below and considered how best to catch a human alone.

The humans that came into town from the road came in groups. Ev's fingers reached over the top of his shoulder to the handle of his longest blade. The blade Jhahgror had named "Kle," "beheading" in the human sounds. Jhahgror had always been delighted in how quickly Ev was able to do this, and when he drew the long blade there was no doubt a Maekmorth would be missing its head before the blade was sheathed again. Ev did not draw Kle without the intent to kill. This was why the other Trolls had called the slightly smaller blade Ev wore at his hip, "Urr", "threat" in the human sounds, though the smaller blade had cleaved its share of leathery flesh. Rarely did he draw the much smaller blades he wore. Ev had given them no names though all the Maekmorth had names for their weapons. The Maekmorth he had been with placed more value on things than other Maekmorth. Ev smiled cruelly, he would prefer to offer Crogar, Crogar's own head in return, but that would not aid him. The other Trolls looked to Crogar in time of crisis, and Ev did not want them looking to him in Crogar's place.

The next group of humans walked past, along with a box of wood set on spinning wheels pulled by a horse. This brought his thoughts back to his problem. Among a group of Maekmorth there was no serious talk but with a single Maekmorth it was possible. With the humans it seemed the same. His fingers tensed around the hilt of Kle. He grimaced. With the Maekmorth it would have been the perfect solution. The Trolls did not care for weaklings that could not fight their own battles. The grimace deepened; he had not been able to fight his own battles until Jhahgror had given him the blades. She had given him Kle before he could lift the big blade. Urr had served until that time. He did not have the physical strength of the other Maekmorth, but with the blades he could be far more deadly. His survival depended on his abnormal speed. His fingers moved away from the hilt of the blade.

Ev was thinking again and that was not considered a healthy habit. Thinking made a Maekmorth hesitate to kill. Thinking was equal to death. Ev shook his head. He had not hesitated in any battle for a long time. The afternoon light glinted off the two teeth he had filed to sharp tips on either side of his upper jaw among the rest of his blunt teeth. The human near Maekmorth hill had run towards him instead of away from him. He had taken this in the same manner he would a grave insult then, but now it gave him an idea. Standing abruptly he left the bushes and strode towards the town. The human whose remains were now settled in six Maekmorth stomachs had told him he was not a Troll. He was about to test that theory in the blunt manner of the Maekmorth, by walking down into the human place in broad daylight.

Roanne came around the corner and stopped dead in her tracks. The laundry basket she had been carrying dropped to the dirt in a huff of dust. Kaylin came around the corner behind her and stopped as well. She could see why Roanne was transfixed by the stranger. Roanne had never been beyond this village, but Kaylin had, and she was not struck by shock at the silver eyes of the tall man who had stopped walking towards Roanne at the sight of Kaylin. The smell was bad and Kaylin never had liked furs, but the stranger's cloak was made of them and his sorry ragged tunic and breeches were made of the darker leather she had witnessed the few trappers from the Scartooth mountain wore. Kaylin sighed in disgust, not knowing why it was the stench and the clothing she always noticed first.

"Roanne?" she looked at the woman transfixed by that silver stare, the stranger's hand was on the hilt of his weapon. "Roanne!"

Roanne did not move. Kaylin took another look at the tall stranger then strode towards him angrily. The sword came free of its sheath but Kaylin was already too close for him to strike, shoving the hand that held the shorter blade to the side and bringing up a hand to push the left side of his face aside. Roanne suddenly felt herself able to move again. She looked at Kaylin in utter astonishment.

"Remember the laundry basket," Kaylin barked, then in a much softer tone. "You might bring some water from the well."

Roanne nodded quickly and disappeared back around the corner from where she had come. The stranger sidestepped, but Kaylin stayed within his guard. She had witnessed enough fighting in the gladiator pits of the city of Bijorth to know it would not be so easy for him to strike at her when she was this close. Kaylin kept the hand to his cheek though he had forced his face around to stare at her. In Bijorth they would have cried witchery at the sight of those silver eyes. Kaylin knew better. Her common-sense brown eyes were not lowered, but she did remove her hand from his cheek.

"You do not belong here," the short woman told him, stepping around and hooking her arm under his elbow.

"I want to talk to..."

"People?" Kaylin asked. "Well, not like that you won't."

The stranger looked a little confused, but he followed her when she guided him around the corner and shoved him into the nearest open doorway past the door Roanne had left ajar. Roanne had gone the other way around towards the well leaving the laundry basket on the floorboards, but Kaylin had no doubt that Roanne would be back in for a peek. The important thing was to get that weapon out of the stranger's hand before Roanne returned.

"You have strange caves," Ev said, peering around at the flimsy furniture, not a single chair had a proper solid base.

Crogar would have smashed them immediately knowing they were useless. Ev waited patiently for the short woman with the brown-red hair to say something. He understood her to be a woman by the long tunic she wore. Jhahgror had shown him a similar tunic when she had spoken of her human pet, but it had been much browner with holes in it. Ev stared at the short woman. The short woman had taken hold of the limb that held the blade and she had not released it. Ev was annoyed at this human but not alarmed. He could easily break away any time he desired. He sniffed her hair. She smelled strange. Not odorous enough to be a good female who did hard labor, and normally gathered the fuel for the cavern fires.

"Caves?" A deep wrinkle appeared between the female's dark eyebrows.

Ev nodded slowly. These were new sounds. He would remember them and practice them later. He did not wish to show off how ignorant he was, and she had not let go of his arm. Ev growled.

The short woman jerked away from him slightly, but she did not let go of his arm. Ev did not understand this. There had been no returning growl, yet she refused to let go! This baffled him but maybe humans did not growl. He had not asked Jhahgror about this. He had always assumed that every animal growled. The short woman leaned in closer. For what purpose? He could only assume she was smelling him. His face flushed a deep red. Among the Maekmorth, close family only smelled each other, others did not dare. Her free hand came up and brushed dirty strands of his hair over his left ear tip. She drew back letting go of his arm to study him, and when she was finished, her hand darted forward to do the same on the right.

"Not bad," she frowned. "You might pass."

"Pass?"

"They might mistake you for human."

"You think I am not!"

"No," the short woman shook her head. "Humans come in many variations with skin colors from dark to light, tall to short, but no human has ears that sharp at the tips."

Ev sat down on the nearest flimsy chair, testing to see whether or not it would hold his weight. Surprisingly it did, but Ev did not trust it to hold him for any length of time. The four spindly supports were too thin.

"What do you think I am?"

"Not a dwarf certainly, and not a Flen," Kaylin laughed. "You are too thin for a Troll, and too short for a Jiant. I would say a centaur but you have no hooves."

Ev's head spun with these new sounds: Centaur, Flen, placed with the same sound of Troll. He had heard dimly of dwarbhes. Nasty little creatures that inhabited the Snowcap mountains far north past the humans. They had fought the Maekmorth in the Scartooth mountains and lost, but that was far before Ev's time. Hearing the chair creak beneath him he stood, thinking it was just a matter of seconds before it would splinter beneath his weight. The chair could not have held Mogrim for the second it would have taken for her to sit down on top of it. The short woman took hold of his arm the second his rear left the chair.

"You need a bath!" she steered him into another room and pointed towards the hollow thing against the wall. "You are too long for it but it will have to do."

Furrows of wrinkles appeared running the length of Ev's forehead. Ev was in trouble.

He had no clue of what she was talking about and that hollow thing had the look of a really narrow bowl. He had never heard of humans eating other humans, or things that looked humanish, but Ev was not so sure. He looked from the hollow thing to the short woman.

"Don't let it scare you, its just a tub," the short woman smiled patting the sides of the tub.

Ev was not reassured but the wrinkles vanished. Looking at him now, she found it hard to remember that they had ever existed on that smooth brow. Taking hold of the crude brooch of iron that held the cloak in place she pulled it free, then tugged it out from under the longer sword sheath that was strapped to his back. She worked quickly and thoroughly taking the great fur cloak into her arms.

"Do you have a name?"

"Ev Vrin," the low growl that started in the back of his throat came forward as did he, catching part of the cloak when it swept off of him and keeping hold of it.

The short woman stared at the two sharp teeth among the dull row he bared at her. She let go of the cloak. Wrinkled folds of gray fur dropped to the floorboards. The folds went taut held up by the corner Ev held in his hand. The woman displayed her dull shining white teeth in a smile.

"You may put it over there," she motioned to a small table that sat nearby.

"Along with the rest of your clothes."

Ev Vrin growled at her, again. Brown eyes glared at him. His silver eyes became slits.

"Do you want to talk to humans or not?" she inquired. "You can leave any time, but if you are going to stay you need to learn to act like a human and what is more, attempt to smell like one!"

Ev stopped growling. He looked at the fur cloak in his hand. He looked at her.

"Ahct?" Ev said the new word but it rolled off his tongue strangely.

This word was one of the few Jhahgror had not taught him and she had been a very thorough teacher. She had always insisted on Ev putting in the and's, the's, of's and all the other little unnecessary nonsense sounds in exactly the right places as a human would. She had drilled him on the ing's, ed's, and s's, but there were some words he had not heard. He shook his head trying to clear it. He had a small head. He could not remember everything.

"Yes, act," the short woman said it for him again. "The more human you are to them, the more they will accept you. When you are strange to them, they fear you, but when you are the same you will be able to walk anywhere except where the rich folk dwell. Their "caves" cannot be entered so easily and you should not be entering the houses of normal folk either without being invited."

Ev took hold of the shaving of leather that held his long sword to his back casting his eyes downward in thought. Kaylin waited, poised over the second bucket that sat on the floorboards near the tub. Her eyes were on him.

"What is it I smell like?"

"A Troll," Kaylin answered honestly. "Though a dung heap might be closer."

"Humans fear this smell?"

Kaylin shook her head and stopped to pick up the empty bucket. "Take my advice, take off your clothes, and get into the tub."

Ev stared at her. Kaylin looked away. Roanne slipped through the door from the outer room and poured the water from her bucket into the tub. She did not miss the opportunity to stare at Ev, but she left on the heels of Kaylin, bound for another trip to the well that was not far away.

Ev stood there watching them go, the short human and the other human with dirt blonde hair. He looked at the tub. He did not see any way of building a fire under it without the gathering of wood and other fuels to stack beneath it. Not a cook pot then, but he did not know what other strange rituals the humans might have. He swung the leather shaving over his shoulder and set Kle on the table. The sword was longer than the table but it did not fall off. Slipping the tunic over his shoulders he threw it over Kle. The bigger shavings of hide he bound his soft feet in were harder to take off. The knots of the smaller leather shavings were weak points in the leather. He broke them hating that he did this, but thinking to himself that the hassle of knotting every leather shaving over again could not be made better by undoing the knots. He had to make repairs on them every so often anyway. He stared down at his soft feet wishing for the thicker leather skin pads on the bottom of every Maekmorth's feet. He left the larger leather shavings lying on the floor. The leather shaving that wound around his waist was next, then the leather beneath it. He paused at the stone that hung around his neck. He would not take it off. Gripping the handle of Urr he drew the blade and left its leather covering on the table. His skin felt funny being free of the hides. Not since his birth had all his skin been left to the open air. His head turned at the knock that sounded at the partially open door. Kaylin waited, then entered when she received no answer. Roanne came in behind her carrying a full bucket of water. Kaylin stopped before Roanne could get past her.

"Not shy are you?" she said out loud, setting her bucket down, and reaching back to take Roanne's.

"Thank you Roanne," she set Roanne's bucket inside too, giving her the third bucket that was empty.

Roanne peered past Kaylin. Ev stared at her. His sword was rising.

"Please, fill this one too," Kaylin muttered, shoving Roanne aside and shutting the door.

Kaylin reached up onto the shelf beside the door and took down a bar of soap. She glanced at Ev. Then she reached up and grabbed another bar of soap.

"Here," she walked over and handed him a soap bar.

Ev took it with his free hand. He looked down at it. Then he looked at her. Kaylin rolled her eyes.

"Don't tell me you do not know how to take a bath."

"Bahth?" Ev Vrin echoed, remembering dimly that Jhahgror had mentioned the word in a comment about how strange human grooming habits were.

Kaylin sighed. Taking him by the arm she guided him over to the tub. Then she released the arm and walked back over to the buckets.

"Step in, sit down," she lifted a bucket.

Ev stepped into the hollow narrow thing. Then he knelt straight down onto it setting his knees against the bottom. He laid Urr in front of him across the thin walls of the tub, but he did not take his hand off the blade.

Kaylin halted, "Lay the sword aside!"

Ev growled. Kaylin set the bucket down. Then she answered with a growl of her own.

"Are you afraid of me?" she accused. "Is that why you keep the blade so close?"

Ev forced himself to set the blade aside. He leaned it upright against the wall. His lip curled in disgust.

"Females!" he snarled, with the exception of Jhahgror, they were always nervous around blades.

Cold freezing water splashed over his head. Ev half rose to a crouch. Two smooth hands pushed him back down by the shoulders. The cold water ran from his skin.

"Males!" Kaylin muttered, then set her hands to scrubbing his back. "This is how you bathe. You scrub the soap against your hide then wash it off with the water. Have you never gone swimming?"

"The M..., I hate water," Ev lied and immediately wished he had not. Long years pretending to be afraid of the water among the Maekmorth who were afraid of water had caused him to say what was not in his heart. He had escaped bullies among the Maekmorth many times by disappearing in the waters beneath the earth and re-emerging in another cavern. It was his secret to keep, but there were times when he kept it too close.

Kaylin laughed. She brought the soap around to his face. Ev took his head away from it spitting into the water. She moved on applying the soap in greater quantities to his smelly hide. She was surprised how easily the mud came away from his hair, (it would not have come away so easily from her own human hair), revealing the white-gold color beneath. Ev squirmed away from the soap in her hands and the hand that tried to keep his limbs where she could work with them.

"Smells bad!" he caught her wrist to keep the offensive substance away from his body.

"Smells human," Kaylin countered. "And it won't be so bad once you wash it off with water!"

Ev's hands dived for the water splashing it on his face and rubbing the disgusting smooth substance off his skin, losing his grip on the other bar of soap, and Kaylin's wrist. Nothing was rough here, not the tub, not the soap, and not Kaylin's hand. Ev had never thought he would miss the feel of rocks on his skin but he missed it now. Everything was too smooth. Shivering with the cold air on his unprotected skin he growled.

The sight of fair spots tinged with red appearing all over what he had tried to make his brown Maekmorth hide, (with the addition of great quantities of mud), made Ev growl louder. Instead of recognizing this to be a warning, Kaylin lifted his chin, shutting it. Then looked down at her work thus far.

"Not bad. You might pass for a human."

Ev wrenched his jaw away, baring his fangs, the sharpened teeth he took great pride in having. What was left of the soap bar she dropped onto his legs. Ev's upper lip curled back in response. Kaylin picked up the other bar of soap.

"You still smell like a Troll," she told him. "And unless this soap is rubbed over every piece of your hide and scrubbed away by the water you will always smell like a Troll and no human will ever talk to you!"

The door opened. Kaylin turned and went to meet Roanne who came in with the next bucket. Kaylin took the bucket from her. She tried to stay in the way of Roanne's view, but Roanne slipped past her taking up the two empty buckets with a wink. Then she was gone out the door again. Kaylin shut it wearily behind her, placing her forearm high up against it and leaning on it for a second. Regarding the bar of soap in her other hand she turned back around with another sigh, knelt down, and placed her right arm over Ev's broad shoulders. She leaned in, intent on scrubbing his chest. Ev's face flushed red, again. Her nose was incredibly close to his skin and she must be smelling him! Ev panicked. He had had to deal with other females before, (and that was unusual considering he was a misborn but misborns received attention when they were the son of a chief), but with the Maekmorth it was simple. Growl and they left. Not leaving gave him the permission to kill, but here, growling seemed to have no effect and she was human! He had no idea whether sniffing this close meant the same thing it did with the Maekmorth. This sent his muddled thoughts spinning but his body was already reacting. His left arm came up under her right armpit latching onto the top of her left shoulder. He sniffed her face. Kaylin jerked back dropping the soap. She stopped twelve inches away, pure shock registering on her face. Ev let go of her tense shoulders immediately. Remembering the wise words of Jhahgror. Jhahgror had indented into his small brain that when a female indicates "no" then there is no going any farther.

"Trolls they..." Kaylin stopped herself. "Like dogs?"

"Your skin smells like soup," Ev stated, looking down into the filthy water below.

"Soap," Kaylin corrected, a slow smile spreading across her face, but it disappeared completely when Ev brought the bar of soap up with his hand and his silver gaze.

Kaylin stood. Ev rubbed the soap against the arm she had already scrubbed, experimenting with the stinky substance. He sniffed it, then wiped it away with water as quickly as possible.

"You are doing fine," Kaylin said, walking towards the door. "Do that all over your body. Wash everything, and growl at anyone who happens to come into the room, besides me, until they go away!"

Ev stared at her for a minute, then began doing what she had said. Kaylin opened the door and shut it again behind her. Walking into the next room she opened the chest at the end of the bed and pulled out a few items. Reaching into the leather pouch hanging from her belt she pulled forth a silver coin and set it atop the rest of the cloths in the chest. Then she shut the lid carefully. Rising, she searched the corners of the room until she found what she was looking for, and replaced it with another coin. Setting the items on the main table she moved to block Roanne's entrance when she came in with the two buckets half full. Roanne stared at her.

"Have you had any trouble?" she asked.

"Yes," Kaylin answered. "But it was not as bad as I feared."

Roanne nodded and handed her the buckets. "He will need the water."

"Will you do me a favor?" asked Kaylin. "And delay Tobar? I do not think he is going to like this."

"I will try," Roanne answered with a frown. "Is it that bad?"

"This could be very bad," Kaylin answered. "Or it might be good news. I do not know and either way I need you to delay Tobar."

"I'll try," Roanne answered. "But he may take a different path back from the hot springs."

Kaylin nodded wishing she could go herself instead of Roanne. She would not miss Tobar no matter what path he took, but it was not a good idea to leave Roanne alone with the stranger without any type of protection. The swords did indeed make Kaylin nervous. Kaylin frowned watching

Roanne leave. Then she hefted the buckets and went in to see how Ev had managed on his own. Her left eyebrow raised once she entered the room. From the looks of things he was doing a fair job. Walking forward quickly she set down the second bucket and dumped the first over him. Setting it down she reached for the second. Ev snorted clearing his nostrils of water. Kaylin brought up the second bucket and splashed it on his face. Ev clutched the side of the tub with both hands. The bits of soap that were left smeared on his fingers. He pushed himself up. Kaylin snatched a clean white cloth from the shelf that hung out from the wall above the tub and draped it over his shoulders.

"Stay," she commanded moving back out of the room to retrieve the items she had taken from Tobar's room.

Kaylin walked back into the bathing room setting down the heavier items and presenting the rest of the items to him. Ev looked down at the clean white cloth tunic and the green breeches. Then he looked back towards his old leather shavings. He had taken up Urr in his hand and looked somewhat ridiculous standing bent over beneath the shelf, with white cloth sliding off his shoulders and the blade in his right hand. Kaylin felt a chill in her bones at the sight of it. Memories of piercing screams were not what she wanted to think about ever. There was a noise behind her. She suspected it was Tobar having returned by a different path than he had used going into the hills, missing Roanne completely. What ill luck. She turned to look. Tobar stood in the doorway to the bathing room.

"What in the nine fire's of Eztar is going on here!" Tobar demanded!

Kaylin sighed. She had been sighing a great deal lately. "This is none of your concern."

Tobar's hard face remained unconvinced. The short dark hair on his head did little to conceal the displeasure in his expression. His weathered skin made him have more the look of a Troll than Ev. Tobar had been handsome once, Kaylin was sure, but the years had scoured his skin in the same way they had scoured what was left of him inside. Kaylin shoved the clothes into Ev's free hand, undid the tie of the small leather bag at her belt, and threw it down at Tobar's feet. The coins inside clinked together drawing Ev's attention, but then why should it not draw a Troll's attention? Kaylin hoped that Ev would not do anything stupid.

Tobar caught up the bag of coins in one quick swipe. Glaring at Kaylin with hard eyes. He did not even bother to give the man a second look. He had never thought this of Kaylin but if she wanted to play games who was he to tell her "no." Her father was long dead and Tobar had never had much respect for him either. Tobar brought up a lone finger to point at Kaylin though he was pronouncing her doom.

"Jotham will not be pleased to learn of this!"

"You will not tell him," Kaylin's voice was low and menacing.

Ev thought the man's reaction rather funny. There was nothing menacing about Kaylin's brown spotted face. He could not understand why the other human was so angry or why he left the bathing room faster than he had come. Ev looked down at Kaylin, setting his sword aside to investigate what she had handed him, showing her he was not afraid. Kaylin looked away from the door the other human slammed shut. She looked down at the tub and the mess of water soaking the floor. Her skin was so warm and without coarse fur. Ev let go of the cloth in his other hand and reached out to touch it. His fingers brushed her cheek curving around the chin and bringing it up. He studied the brown dots on her pale cheeks.

"You look more Troll than I do," Ev gave her a compliment.

Kaylin laughed swatting away his hand. "Thank you for the flattery...I think?"

"You have brown..." Ev stopped unable to find the right word in the human language, and not certain there was one for this in the language of the Trolls.

"Freckles?" Kaylin supplied.

Ev made a funny face trying to say the word. "Freakhals?"

"Freckles," Kaylin said again. "Some people do have brown dots on their faces and some people like them."

Ev's right hand moved up her left arm. Kaylin placed a hand on his chest and pushed him away or she tried to. Ev was used to being shoved around by those much larger than him but none had shoved him around since the time he had learned the use of the blades. This woman was not larger than Ev, she was shorter, and human. Kaylin's hand met with a hillside of solid muscle. Kaylin looked up into his eyes. Then she wished she had not. Breaking free of his stare was harder than breaking free of the light hold he had on her arm, but she was too wise to be caught in that silver stare. Ev was going to have enough trouble fitting in with humans. He did not need any other kind of trouble, yet.

"Get dressed, I will be back in soon," Kaylin walked away.

Ev looked down at the tunic and sniffed it. There was the definite smell of soap. He threw it over his head anyway, it made him itch. The tunic was too soft. Hide was better. The other piece was of the same softness and it would offer little protection to his legs should anyone try to bite them. He placed the cloth pants on but he, also, took up the crude hide of the kind he had always worn and slid his legs into the leather. The feet wraps would be next. Ev groaned inwardly. Taking up the biggest hide shaving he began wrapping his left foot on the edge of the small table. Kaylin rolled her eyes when she reentered. She made a few adjustments and grabbing up the worn boots she had dropped on the floor, she handed them to him, the leather shaving dropped into the small lake of muddy bath water beneath the tub. Ev grunted, irritated that she would interrupt him when he was doing something difficult.

"These are boots! You place them on your feet," Kaylin explained in a low voice.

"You should hurry. Strange things tend to happen when Tobar is vexed."

Ev did not hurry. It took time to figure out how boots fit on feet. Kaylin stood to the side impatiently tapping her fingers on her wider hard leather belt. Once the boots were on his feet Ev reached for the gray fur cloak on the table and his weapons. Kaylin frowned.

"Leave them. Human's do not take kindly to blades, especially of that kind," Kaylin warned. "You do not need them, and we will be back."

Ev took up Urr with the smaller blades that hung from the belt. Kaylin growled. Ev glanced up. She pointed to two of the blades that were most definitely not of human make. Ev cut them from the makeshift belt with the third plain blade. Then he hid them in the outer sides of the boots he now wore. Ev tied the belt around the tunic at his waist in spite of Kaylin's protests that he would not need it.

Kaylin stopped finding reasons for him to leave the blades here when it became clear he was not taking the biggest of his blades. Kaylin looked at Urr and decided she could live with it. The blade was not made by human hands but it was plainer and she hoped people would not look too closely. Ignoring the mess on the floor she took his arm and guided him out into the outer room. There she sat him down in a chair and left him. Tobar, who was seated in another of the flimsy chairs by the wall looked up long enough to glare at Ev before going back to carving the wood in his hand with a very small, very sharp knife. Ev shifted uneasily. The chair creaked beneath him, he moved to get his feet under him but Kaylin was there immediately pushing him back down by the shoulders.

"It will not break," she leaned over him. "I promise."

Ev settled back into the chair awaiting the crash to the floor he knew was imminent. Kaylin took hold of his white-gold hair and placed the brush in her hand to the edges of the locks being extremely careful not to yank on them. Her hands were careful.

"So tell me what you know about Trolls," said Kaylin anticipating the start that brought him halfway out of the chair.

Kaylin wore a grim smile when he yowled unable to leave the seat with his hair held captive in her hands. This time she did yank on it, hard. Ev's rear hit the chair again and his hand closed over the hilt of his blade. The startled yowl of pain became a dangerous growl. Kaylin swirled around half onto his lap stopping him from drawing the blade with her right hand on his wrist. The other hand kept tight hold on his hair. Kaylin was stronger than Ev had thought but he knew he could throw her off whenever he chose. The problem was that this close, beneath the smell of soap, the true smell of her skin was intoxicating. He tried to concentrate on the smell of the soap but it was hard.

Tobar cast down the wood carving onto the pile of shavings on the floor and stood. His face had become more ugly than it had been when he had walked in and first seen Ev. The point of the knife blade shook towards Kaylin.

"Do whatever you want when I am not here, but do not dare jump him in front of my eyes!" the anger in Tobar's voice exploded outward, but he did not remain to see Kaylin's reaction. He stalked into the back room instead leaving the door to crash shut behind him.

Kaylin stared after Tobar, thinking for a moment. Then she continued brushing out the tangles of Ev's hair. Ev's hand remained on Urr but he did not draw the blade.

"Listen closely," said Kaylin. "Growling is not something you should ever do when talking to humans. Speak less, and listen more. Ask questions with great caution, and never draw your blade unless someone is about to kill you."

"Why do you give me orders?" Ev growled.

"Take my "orders" or go wander around on your own," Kaylin's answer was clipped. "You will probably end up dead but do whatever you want, I am just offering you my advice."

Kaylin finished, making certain the tips of his ears were covered by his hair, and setting aside the brush. Ev rose from the creaking chair and Kaylin turned to look at him. Assessing him with overcritical eyes the edges of her mouth slipped downward.

"If you are planning to stay here for any amount of time, I would cut the hair."

Ev grabbed hold of the tip of a lock and took a look grimacing at its white coloring. The gold tint was barely noticeable and not anywhere near the darker colors of Maekmorth hair. His lip curled up over his teeth. Kaylin stepped forward grabbing an arm and opening the door she guided him out of the house into the street.

"Try not to stare at anyone, especially females," Kaylin advised him then grinned. "Oh, and don't snarl. It's not very becoming."

Tobar heard Kaylin shut the door behind her. This brought him into the outer room. Stretching out his left hand palm upward, fingers curved, he spoke a word of magic. The outline of a blue sphere filled his hand. He studied it noting where the blue faded into purple and eventually to red on a certain side. Tobar turned towards the direction the red was and followed it until the entire sphere was a bright red that pained human eyes. Tobar blinked letting the water in his eyes soothe his eyeballs and reminding himself that this must be done. He had come to a stop in the bathing room. Ignoring the severe ache that was spreading through his left arm he brought his other hand to the table lifting the gray fur hide. Shoving the back of his left hand, (the hand that held the sphere), into the sheath of the blade he drew it with his right, carefully, and laid it back on top the fur.

The light of the sphere bathed the blade on the fur in crimson, but the blade absorbed the light from the sphere and the rest of the dim light in the room. Tobar's hand clenched crushing the sphere into red sparks. The blade was pure black. Tobar cursed under his breath. He had spent a fourth of his life hunting this blade and now when he did not want to see another black blade again, it had come into his house.

Bringing out a dark cloth he took the blade from the fur careful not to touch it. He left the glowing glyph of shifting around the glyph of lightning in place of the sword. The blue glyph of shifting drew power from the lightning solidifying it into a mass the same weight and appearance of the sword once laid out on the fur.

There were six swords altogether. Six made, four destroyed. Ardenvale had destroyed the first and the third. Shevelstead the second. Tobar himself had aided Koratin when he destroyed the fourth upon the death of Master Sharin. Maywarin had thrown the fifth into a volacano. His hand fell against the table steadying himself. It may not be a Seeker. It could be a magical black blade, nothing more. There was only one way to know. Unsheathing his small sharp knife he held his free hand over the blade and pricked the tip of his finger with its thin point. The bead of blood that dripped from it fell towards the blade with a speed that surpassed gravity. Striking the blackness the blood flowed over the blade until its color was dark red. Tobar gave a yell that was swallowed by the dark red glow of the blade, and was struck cold. He fell down against the floorboards momentarily drained, knowing he could not destroy it and live. Already it had weakened him and the blade had not drunk the blood of a human mage for a very long time...

## Ch. 3 "Who's Dis?"

"Where are you taking me?" asked Ev Vrin.

"To Brad Den's house," Kaylin said guiding him over the rocky road to a house on the outskirts of the town.

People stared at him but then they were bound to stare. Anyone with Kaylin was bound to be interesting. Kaylin was one of the few who had traveled far beyond the town limits and that in itself raised eyebrows. The trapper Mekginis and Ron Derath the tinker were the only other people in this town who traveled on a regular basis. Some said Tobar had traveled at one time but though he looked strong enough, his travel years were long past. He had been here for fifteen years and he fit into their town so well that no one remembered when he had not been there. Kaylin was different. She was the light talk of the town. No one had any doubts that wherever she passed she would leave a tale from a far off land or two. The town children loved her for this and one young boy who came running up from the Brad Den place demanded to hear one the moment he sighted Kaylin down the road.

"Kaylin, do you have a tale for us!"

Kaylin smiled when the young boy broke into a full speed run. They walked no faster down the road that was set between the hills and the plains with the town at their back, but they did not need to. They were nearly to the homestead and the boy ran up to them without any great mishap, though Kaylin had feared he might trip he was running so fast.

"Kaylin...Kaylin," the young boy was out of breath but Kaylin messed up his hair and told him to take a breath before speaking.

"You are here!" his smile knew no limits. "It's been...its been..."

"A long time," Kaylin finished for him. "I know Benjamin, but I've been to Bijorth and back and you know how long that takes.

"Oh, but Kaylin you always say that!"

"Because its true," Kaylin answered his disappointment. "I always stop off at Bijorth on my way here."

Benjamin tried to think of how far the city was compared to how long Kaylin had been gone. Bijorth was across the Golden Plains on the other side of the Ram. The Ram was a mountain pass that was guarded by the ancient race of dwarves and it was said there were things in those mountains no human wished to see. This was a journey that may have taken her that long without including any other interesting stops.

"This is Ev," Kaylin introduced the tall man beside her and Benjamin eyes widened as he craned his neck back to look up at the man.

"Is he from Bijorth?" asked Benjamin, thinking he must be one of the great barbarians that sometimes came to trade in that great city and remained there earning a living by fighting in the gladiator pits. Kaylin had told tales of this last time she had come to Brad Den much to his mother's dismay.

Kaylin laughed gently, messing his hair a second time. "No, Benjamin. He's never been this far north I think."

"You mean you live in the Scartooth Mountains?" asked Benjamin staring up at Ev. "In the south...where they used to say there were...Trolls?"

Ev stared down at him unsure exactly how to answer that question. Kaylin watched him carefully. She had smelled Maekmorth on him and his manners were no better than a Troll's but did he truly know the Maekmorth, aside from sharing their smell?

"Mama says they grind your bones and eat you alive," Benjamin continued on to Ev's relief and Kaylin's disappointment. "She says a Troll will eat anything!"

"Is that true?" Ev asked, (thinking that no Troll he knew would be able to stomach that smelly stuff the humans called soap, so there were things they would not eat). Benjamin gave a tiny jerk at the two sharpened teeth Ev had displayed by opening his mouth to speak.

"Wow," Benjamin backed up a pace. "Are those real? Is he a werewolf, Kaylin?"

"No," Kaylin laughed kneeling down to place a hand on his shoulder reassuringly.

"I would never bring a werewolf to meet your ma and pa."

"Then how come his teeth are that way?"

"I have not asked him, yet." Kaylin replied, standing back up but keeping that hand on

Benjamin's shoulder. "But my guess would be that he filed them down. Am I correct?"

Ev nodded trying to keep the questionable teeth out of sight. He had not thought they would be a problem but now he was beginning to see why Kaylin was so concerned that he act human. He could not understand how a human child could be scared by something so small as fangs and not even proper fangs! He wondered what the child would think of Mogrim's set. She kept them so long they grew out of her mouth and up by her nose from the lower jaw, the upper fangs had been knocked out by an over-eager Troll chief or so she claimed.

Farther down the road there was a wooden sign with the words "The Brad Den Stead" and a picket fence. Benjamin quickly opened the gate to lead them through. Inside the yard chickens pecked and flapped with so much violence they caused Ev to lay his hand to Urr. The woman who came out of the house was no less short than Kaylin and quite plump. She held a babe in her arms and a jolly expression on her face that became a look of delight upon spotting Kaylin.

"Kaylin darling! It's okay, Linette," she glancing quickly behind her, then she stepped down the porch with a speed slowed only for the baby's sake. "Where have you been?"

"And who is this?" asked the young woman, Linette, coming around hehind the older woman setting aside the axe when she saw Kaylin. "Not another idiot who has come to rob us, is it?"

"No, this is Ev." Kaylin remembered hearing something about the old drunk Marny coming by to rob folks before but she doubted he had gotten anything from the Brad Den place. Her eyes went back to the babe. "Now this can't be the little bairn I saw you with before I left."

The woman laughed. "Of course, 'tis not. That little bairn has grown greatly since you left, and, ah, there she is...light of my eyes."

The small girl that came around the side of the building ran away from the chickens and came to a stop in front of Ev. Her reddish curls bobbed up and down with the remembrance of the run. Ev looked down at her. She held up her arms.

"We named her Kaylin Joy after you," the woman smiled. "So she won't be afraid to travel like you do when she grows up."

"I think she wants to be picked up, Ev," Kaylin commented at the same time though she did not miss the woman's words and turned back towards her with a reply of her own."I am deeply flattered that you decided to name her after me."

"Ah well, twas the perfect name," the woman replied modestly. "You've the luck of good times, I fancy, and we want Kaylin Joy to have more than a bit of that."

Ev lifted Kaylin Joy up into his arms much to the surprise of a pursuing rooster. The rooster pecked at his leg but Ev's kick sent it flying. Benjamin's eyes grew wide for the third time. He peered up at Ev. Linette looked shocked.

"Blimey," Benjamin gasped. "Do you always do that to roosters?"

"Ev," Kaylin said sharply. "That animal belongs to these people. It's not a good idea to damage other people's things unless you are willing to pay for them and even then it is still not a good idea."

Ev stared at her uncomprehendingly. How could this animal be theirs when it was still walking around living? When you killed something, then it was yours, not before. Otherwise the living animal could not belong to anyone, not when the animal was still running around on two legs. Unless it was a pet and he did not see a chain.
Ev stared at the little human in his arms. The little one had on the biggest smile he had ever seen. Her tiny fingers pulled on his long locks.

"Who's Dis?"

"Ev Vrin," Kaylin replied instantly.

The little girl frowned. "Eb Bin!"

"She is just learning to talk, Ev," Kaylin warned.

"Yes, and mighty good at it she is becoming too," proclaimed Kaylin Joy's mother.

"Yes, I can hear that," Kaylin answered keeping her eyes on Ev. "She looks healthy, Hanna."

"Eb Bin! Eb Bin!" the little girl knocked his smooth nose with her small hand until this hand too, discovered the silky strands of his hair.

Ev Vrin was too surprised to growl. With an effort he kept his jaw from falling open to reveal the two sharpened teeth the boy was scared of before. The red curls bounced on the little girl's head when she laughed, delighted to be lifted by someone new and so tall. Her blue eyes could see for a long ways all the way past the horse pasture. Her little face glowed with happiness.

"Oh yes, the dear! She is that! Not a sick day in her life, I'd have to say. Taking after you I believe she is. I've never heard of you being sick before."

"Well, I have been," Kaylin answered not telling the full truth, she had been sick with fear in the time of her father, in the time that the Essenceater Ghosts had haunted the land.

"Then she takes after her uncle Edgar I shouldn't wonder," Hanna replied stoutly. "He's had maybe a month at the most of sick days in his life. There weren't a time last year that he were down with anything even when the flu swept through, why he..."

"When is Uncle Edgar coming back?" Benjamin asked.

Hanna sent a worried glance towards the man who had walked up from the stables. Stout and tall Kaylin would never wish to see his angry side. The man frowned catching the last few sentences of the conversation.

"He should have been back by now. Threadshire is not that far," he said, giving the greeting of a nod to Kaylin.

"You don't think Trolls got him do you?' asked Benjamin.

"Trolls? Benji!," Linette swept forward to her younger brother clipping him smartly across the hair, and causing no damage. "They're fairytales. There are no such things!"

Kaylin opened her mouth but Hanna gave her a hard glare. "That's right, there are no such things. Now Benjamin you had best get to your chores."

"Yes, ma'am," Benjamin started off towards the barn but the stout man's hand brought him back around by the shoulders.

"Kaylin, have you seen Edgar," he asked knowing she might well have come around through Threadshire.

Bijorth she may have been through but he had known Kaylin for years, long enough to know she did not always travel in a straight line. She did not always come from the direction she said she had come from though there was no doubt she had been to Bijorth. She had brought things to trade with that a human could not find around here, things not made in any human kingdom. The same things the merchants brought from the great cities. He did not question her about her journeys but he understood that Bijorth was not the only place she had traveled, though it was the one she was quickest to name whenever anyone asked her where she had been most recently.

"No, I was thinking you might know more being on the border," Kaylin answered, the lines had come back between her eyebrows. "The deer are fleeing to the north, there may come a day soon when we must follow the deer and the birds."

"Well," Hanna gave her a brave smile. "I can't imagine anything would have happened to him on the road."

"Could I go, Mom?" asked Benjamin. "It's not that far, just past Maekmorth hill, and I could see Aunt Beth and take her some of the jam you made."

"No," several voices answered at once drawing Linette's attention.

"That's more than half a days journey," complained Hanna.

"If anyone needs to go, I will go," said the stout man.

"It is not safe," Kaylin turned her hard gaze on Hanna and the stout man.

"I will not let him go," the stout man promised. "But Edgar is late."

"Brad," there was a soft warning in Kaylin's voice. "I don't want you on that road either."

Brad stepped forward patting Benjamin to help him on his way to the barn but Benjamin did not go, "You do know something then."

"Only that it is not safe," replied Kaylin. "Edgar..."

"My goodness," Hanna exclaimed. "You are looking a bit green Ev, are you ill?"

Kaylin Joy punched the locks of hair aside on his left revealing the point tipped ear. Her eyes became rounder than blue berries. Her small head blocked the sight from the other family members but Kaylin saw it and quickly reached for her.

"Kaylin Joy," she called taking her from Ev's arms. "Do you remember me?"

"Ribhons!" Kaylin Joy cried, the last time Kaylin had come she had dangled beautiful ribbons of different colors for Kaylin Joy to touch.

"That's right," Kaylin smiled at her, "I brought ribbons for you and your sisters."

Ev moved away from the humans in a quick stride bound for the other side of the house. Linette followed. Then Kaylin caught sight of her.

"Are you alright, mister," Linette called, but Ev did not answer.

"Linette!" Kaylin said sharply, causing the young woman to turn. "Would you take Kaylin Joy, I think she has had enough of being held by strangers."

Ev disappeared around the edge of the building. The baby began to cry. Hanna took her immediately into the house followed by Linette who took Kaylin Joy. The young child was not at all ready to be moved but they managed, especially with her father's three sentence lecture on about how she should not be going up to strangers and asking them to pick her up. They could be dangerous. Brad paused after opening the door for all the women save Kaylin. He looked at her then let it swing shut.

"What do you know that we do not?" Brad's expression was grim.

"I don't know anything," Kaylin answered looking past Benjamin who was peering around the corner where Ev had disappeared. "yet."

"Who is the man you brought?" Brad demanded.

"I don't know," Kaylin walked towards Benjamin, peered around the corner above him, then she walked around it leaving Brad with this advice. "Stay here."

Brad turned, opened the door in disgust and went in to find his wife. There was no getting anything out of Kaylin when she was in this mood. He would convince her to tell him later but right now she was too distracted to listen.

"Benjamin, the chores," he commanded right before the door slammed shut.

Ev had fallen on his knees against the hillside. *The head of the human hung from the tree half devoured.* Ev shut his eyes hoping the darkness would vanish the memory. His body heaved. He had a small stomach. he had always had a small stomach. His jaws parted, saliva came out in a dry heave he could not stop. He had not eaten. Not today, not yesterday but his stomach was small. He did not need so much food. *Flesh was torn from the bones and stuffed between huge Maekmorth fangs. Qwar turned to make a joke to Croager about how delicate and tender the meat was compared to mountain goat.* He had not eaten. The heaves wracked his body again. He had not eaten. His hand clawed the dirt of the hillside.

*"When is Uncle Edgar coming back?"* he remembered the young male asking. *"...just past Maekmorth hill..."*

"What is it?" Kaylin's strong voice cut into his memories. "What is it you know?"

She grabbed his shoulder and shoved him over onto his back. Ev stared at her, his breath heaving within his lungs, jaws agape. The crinkle in her brow was deep.

"Edgar's not coming back, is he?"

Ev threw himself over onto his knees and shook his head. Kaylin knelt down in front of him placing a hand on his bowed back. She smoothed the cloth over it.

"You have to tell me what happened," she coaxed Ev.

Ev shook his head a second time, violently. Kaylin moved away. The hand slid from Ev's back.

"Ev!"

"Eaten," Ev looked up, the whites of his eyes were red rimmed. "Ask no more."

"Ev," she grabbed both shoulders and shook him. "I need to know. How many?"

Ev held out his hands. His fingers were extended. Easy for him to count. "Ten. More than ten."

"More than ten?" Kaylin sat back letting go of him. "Maekmorth. That is what you mean isn't it? The Maekmorth are coming."

Ev brought his toes under his legs and lifted to his feet pointing towards the house, "They must leave."

Kaylin nodded slowly bringing herself back to her feet at this demand. She did not look back at the house. Kaylin fixed her stare on Ev instead.

"How many?" she asked again.

"How many?" Ev echoed in quiet rage. "The Maekmorth have come to take back their land."

"How many Maekmorth," Kaylin had a quiet rage of her own. "One clan, two clans? Is it a raiding party or is it Grael himself that comes?"

"This is Maekmorth land," Ev growled. "You, all of you, must leave or you will be eaten."

"Including you Ev?"

Ev looked to the side. He could not meet her silvery gaze. His own silver eyes clenched shut.

"This is not Maekmorth land. The elves were here before the humans, before the dwarves, before the Maekmorth!" Kaylin's whisper was fierce.

"The Maekmorth found this land empty!" Ev snapped allowing the snarl welling up in his gut to come out, his silver eyes slit open to glare at her.

"The elves were there before the Maekmorth," Kaylin met the glare with a glare of her own. "And they bequeathed this land to the humans!"

Ev's snarling voice took on the more guttural sounds of the Maekmorth creating a horrible accent that would have frightened a smaller human. "Then let these...elves fight Maekmorth!"

Kaylin's mouth dropped open, her eyes went wide. She straightened. Then she blinked.

"Where have you been?" She stared at him for a minute studying his face to see whether or not he meant what he had just said. "You do not know? You really don't know?"

The snarl in the back of Ev's throat had taken over. He was frustrated with this female beyond any other human and he could not make her understand. His fingers gripped the handle of Urr.

"How could you not know?" Kaylin's mouth fell open, but she shut it again quickly.

"Know what?" Ev roared.

Ev was close, very close to losing all use of human sounds. His brain coursed with rage, not with the knowledge Jhahgror had taught him. Kaylin blinked, her face went through several expressions Ev did not recognize or care to. Then she turned her back on him and began to walk away.
The blade slid from its leather shavings. Two steps and he swung it at her neck intent on stopping the blade just short of her throat in order to allow her to see what he could do to her should she refuse to answer the question. Urr's sharp edge did not stop short of Kaylin's neck, it stopped short of empty air. The growl that throbbed through Ev's chest did not prevent him from swinging his sword back from the stopping point in midair now that there was nothing there. His teeth gnashed together. He scanned the space that lay between him and the house and jerked his head around trying to find Kaylin, his eyes grew wider with shock. There was nothing there. Birds called in the trees above. Ev looked up at them and snarled. The sparrow closest fled the branch it had been perched on. Behind Ev the cat that had been sitting on the back porch ran for the barn. Beneath his shadow a mole scurried through the underbrush. He looked back towards the house. The boy was watching. Ev growled at the boy, too!

## Ch. 4 Roanne's Fear

Roanne crept into the room very much afraid but she did not know what it was she feared. She had felt this fear before long ago. Longer than her memory stretched, before the accident. She was seven. She did not remember any time before she was seven. Most people had memories of when they were a child and some had memories of when they were a babe. Brief flashes or feelings, but Roanne had nothing. Nothing past seven, and she had not asked Tobar about this. This fear was the reason. She could feel it growing with every step. Sheer terror assaulted her senses until she found it too hard to take another step. Her eyes wandered the dark rooms. This was not like Tobar to keep it this dark. Always there was a candle, always there was light. Had Tobar not come back? Was Kaylin okay? Had the stranger done something to her? Anger rose in the bottom of her stomach at this thought. No one should hurt Kaylin, but had something been done. Then who was she to fight it? Roanne crouched unmoving until her eyes adjusted to the darkness and she saw Tobar on the floor of the bathing room. His body was convulsing. Roanne gasped. His back arched, and hunched shaking the supports of the table when his arm struck them. There was something heavy on top of that table glowing a faint red but Roanne ignored it running forward to aid her father.

Tobar did not acknowledge her. She pulled him away from the table's legs, making certain he was able to breath, dodging his suddenly flailing limbs. His eyes stared without knowing whom he saw. Roanne bit her lip. Tears formed in her eyes. This was the reason Tobar could not work at a trade. This was the reason he bathed in the springs every morning or evening, (when he missed the mornings). Kaylin brought medicine. She always brought medicine but nothing had worked. The elixir they had bought from the merchants who came through on their way to Bijorth had not worked either. She had begged him to let her take up a trade, to do something, anything that would aid them, but Tobar had refused. He was her father as far as he was concerned and he would provide for her. This had led to all sorts of strange boarders over the years. Kaylin was the only boarder Roanne trusted. Tobar kept close watch over all boarders save Kaylin. Where was Kaylin? Roanne stared at the long thing that glowed atop the table. The fear flared in her gut. That was it. That was where the fear was coming from and she did not want to know what kind of magic was set therein. Tobar's seizure ceased abruptly. His head thumped against the floor. Roanne gathered Tobar into her lap resting his head on a much softer surface. The crook of her elbow was not that soft but compared to the floor it was better. Tobar's eyes flicked wide.

"Roanne...sword..." he mumbled and muttered but she could make out little of it. Leaning closer she listened harder.

"You don't touch the sword," Tobar swept his fingers around in a magic circle bringing hers around with his, until his eyes regained the focus they needed, then he sat up and took Roanne by the shoulders. "Listen, you must not touch the sword."

Roanne shivered. Tobar nodded as though he expected that response. There was the possibility that he was not her father. Roanne shivered a second time knowing her memories did not go that far back, but he always knew what was best.

"You must take the vial out from under the broken floorboards by the corner of my bed," Tobar continued.

Roanne nodded wordlessly. This was serious. Tobar was not this serious unless there was great danger. She rose and went to fetch it. The floorboards were old and left splinters in her soft fingers but she pried them apart and took hold of the glass vial beneath. Tobar was standing when she came back into the bathing room but his fingers clutched the edges of the table.

"Roanne, listen carefully," Tobar told her. "You must take the white cloth from the shelf. The lowest one beneath the rest and wrap the sword in it but do not let it touch your skin, for the love of El! Do not let it touch your skin!"

Roanne set the vial on the table and numbly took the cloth from beneath the chest. Folding it over the sword she picked it up carefully by its handle. Red light shown though the white cloth. Tobar took it from her, keeping his hands always on the cloth. He tucked it beneath his arm. His left hand came back to the table atop the fur. The fur rose beneath it. Roanne looked into Tobar's aged face hoping he would leave this and go to bed where he belonged after a fit that great, but there was not much hope of this. When Tobar had it in his mind to do something, he would do it, no matter the cost.

"Take up the vial, Roanne," he looked at her. "But do not drop it! Not if you stumble! Not if you trip! Do not drop it!"

Roanne did what Tobar urged her to do and more. Tobar was a father to her and he had never done anything to harm her. Roanne trusted him above Kaylin, and followed him when he walked from the room, out of the house, and into the dark street.

## Ch. 5 Human Beings. Growl

Ev walked through the hills circling around the human dwellings in the same way he had done when first he had sighted them, until he was on the other side of town. Urr was gripped in his left hand and there was blood on it. Three long brown feathers sticky with blood were stuck in his belt. He had a small stomach but Mogrim was right. Not eating made him weak. His body would not have heaved so in front of Kaylin had it not been weak from lack of eating. His stride carried him back into town, back to the house Kaylin had taken him to. Kaylin was not there. The house was empty and dark. Ev stopped in the middle of the outer room. He walked past the door shoving it aside to the table where his things lay. Untying his belt with his right hand he let it fall. He listened. Nothing. Placing Urr beside his gray fur cloak he grabbed the soft tunic on his back and pulled it off. The smooth cloth tickled his back. Ev threw it onto the floor leaving the three bloody feathers with it. Then he took up his hide tunic and placed it over his bare skin. He took up the lower belt and retied it over the hide tunic. Sheathing Urr he flipped aside the gray fur cloak to lay his hands on the longer blade, Kle. His fingers tingled at the touch of its handle. Bringing it upwards towards his nose he sniffed it. Tobar! That was the human's smell. He drew it trying to see what the human had done.

The black blade was whole and sharp. Ev tested its blade with his finger. The blade's edge drew blood. The blood dripped down the tip of the blade and fell onto the floorboards when he lowered it. Slinging the second belt over his shoulder Ev wondered why Tobar had handled the blade. Why had the human not stolen it or broken it? What good would handling it do? The cloak came next. Ev had a time piercing it with the crude brooch a second time but he managed, always pausing to listen every ten seconds. When he was finished he took up Kle and walked into the center of the outer room. Tobar's scent was strong on the blade. Too strong! He could not smell the metal beneath. Raising the sword Ev brought it down cleaving the flimsy chair in his way into pieces. The sword sparked. Ev frowned. Crackling blue charges of lightning ran the length of the blade. Ev waited. The charges vanished. Two shallow grooves appeared betwixt Ev's eyebrows. The corner of his mouth slid upward his right cheek in a grim grin. Were this all the damage Tobar had done to it, Ev could live with it. The smallest sliver of smoke drifted up from a severed chair leg. Having a sword with lightning in it might even impress Grael! No matter the singed fingers. Ev grimaced. When he was certain all of the lightning was gone he sheathed the blade.

The cold night air struck his face when he creaked the door open that led into the street. Ev smiled coldly. He did not know where Kaylin was but he would find Tobar. Tobar he could track. He sniffed the air. Unlike Kaylin his scent had not vanished. The other human woman was with Tobar. The scents were a muddled mess here in town but all he needed to do was stay with the right scent until it left the road. He crouched down to look at the ground finding fresh tracks in the dust. He walked then cautious not to confuse them with any of the other tracks beneath. The street here was empty but farther down it was not. Four young men leaned against an old wooden pole that was set into two shorter wooden posts in front of a building that a great amount of noise was coming out of. The tracks led by them into the light that shown from the windows of the building. Ev walked the tracks half in a crouch, to make certain he did not lose them, and half in the manner a man would walk creating a funny half illusion of what he was in the shadows.

"Wolf!" the boy to the left shouted and pointed.

"Wolf?" the second biggest laughed, and the larger boy to the right howled. "That ain't no wolf!"

"Looks like a wolf to me," the boy on the right said, stepping into the street trying to get a better look.

The second biggest jumped away from the post, bent down, and snatched a rock form the roadside, "That ain't no wolf and I'll prove it!"

The second biggest boy pitched the rock at the shape. He was not the best thrower in the group but his arm had muscle to it and his aim was not bad. Intent on the tracks beneath his nose Ev did not see it. The rock thudded into his shoulder. Ev snarled from the pain and shock that the puny little human would do this.

"Not a wolf at all! What is it, ya think?"

"Grab another rock, and let's find out!" shouted the biggest of the boys snatching up another rock and pitching it at Ev, Ev dodged it easily now that he was aware of the pests.

"Yeah, come on," cried the boy with the brown hair who carried the crude short sword his father had given into his keeping to care for during the time he was inside. "Let's see whether it bleeds!"

They rushed no closer than three yards when the shape rose up from its crouch and threw the fur cloak aside displaying two sharp teeth amidst the duller humanish teeth. A wild snarl sent the youths back a few steps, but when the wicked blade, that was bigger and sharper than the dull crude short sword in possession of the boy with brown hair, was slipped out of the sheath they ran. The second biggest boy was stupid enough to pitch one last rock at the shape that was now hunting them! The rock hit Ev's leg. Ev grunted at the momentary pain but he kept after the boy, darting past the others when the boy broke away from them running through the alleyway, and up into the bushes of the hill. There he lay low in the brush thinking he was safe. Ev passed him there, circled around, and pulled the youth up by his hair from behind. Finding Urr's tip at his throat the youth screamed.

Ev smiled cruelly. This was a good beginning. The youth held out his hands.

"Please, don't. Please! I didn't know you were a human. I thought you were a wolf!" he cried.

Human! Ev paused at the word. Yanking the youth around he stared at the human youngling's face. The human's eyes were wet. Looking down Ev could see they were not the only place on the human that was wet. He withdrew Urr back to his shoulder, but did not let go of the human's hair. Thinking was a bad thing, he lamented, when he stared at the boy he thought of how he himself had felt when Crogar lifted him off his own feet in the caves. The sword arced through the air its keen edge cleaving into the thin strands of the little human's hair. The youth fell against the hillside and lay there with shorter hair, crumbled, and wet but still living. Ev sheathed Urr and stepped over him disappearing in to the bushy shadows of the night.

Roanne gasped for breath. Tobar was out of air too, but the stubborn man would not admit it. She looked up at his crouched form leading the way in the darkness with his sphere of light cast before him and the long thin thing wrapped in white beneath his armpit. She carried the vial always before her, being careful where she stepped, and she made sure she had a firm hold on it. Tobar walked up the trail with the knowledge of every twist and bend. Roanne had not been up it more than two or three times. Tobar had shown her the way twice but she had refused to go there after their second trip. The third time she had gone when Tobar had not come home, but she had not gone all the way up to the springs that day. She had found Tobar halfway up laying by the side of the road too weakened by a seizure to move. That had scared her. Tobar was all she had and there was no other family she remembered.

There was no one else likely to take her save Brad and Hanna but they had four children already! She would be in the way she was certain, and Hanna already disliked her. Spells they said. The gossipers accused her of working spells and what could she say to that? What could she say when it was true? Tobar had given her a book of magic on her thirteenth birthday. She had been working minor enchantments ever since, none of the hard stuff mark thee, but enough to know how to deal with the hard stuff in theory should the need ever arise. Tobar had been a great mage she believed. There had been a time. It was in the stories he told. He never said it and Kaylin never said it but in his stories Tobar had feared nothing, and no small magic caster would have had that kind of bravery unless they were stupid. Tobar did not strike Roanne as stupid. More stubborn than fifty mules, this she could see, but not stupid.

Tobar had always held that half his tales of great mages and magical things were not true but Roanne did not believe him. She had not believed him since the day she caught Kaylin telling a similar tale to the one he had told her a week ago. The difference in this tale was the viewpoint. The mage who had defeated the wooden Chimera was not some fool of a hedge mage but a mage of great power who had studied under the great headmaster who was elven. Roanne had asked her the name of the mage and Kaylin had laughed wondering aloud how it was that Tobar had never told her, and when Roanne had expressed her confusion Kaylin had muttered something about stubborn old relics. She would say no more though Roanne asked her. Roanne had been curious about whether Tobar had been one of the seven, she had tried to peg him in Bijorth the night of Forging when the earth had trembled with the powers unleashed, but Tobar never admitted to anything.

Tobar did not look that old, but it would explain his seizures. No mage who had lived through the night within the circle of seven had come away whole and uninjured. Two had been blasted to ash and the other four had barely escaped with their lives. The Essenceater Ghosts had taken them it was rumored, but six warriors of the north had destroyed the Essenceater Ghosts that very same night.

"All rats in a great large trap," Tobar used to say of all involved. "Spun by elves."

"Was it really the fault of the elves?" Roanne remembered asking.

Tobar had laughed and ruffled her long hair. "Now don't you believe anything you hear about the elves, you hear?"

Roanne had not, from that day forward. They said the elves had made the Essenceater Ghosts to kill the other races, but the human mages had driven them from the earth and with the aid of the six warriors they had destroyed the Essenceater Ghosts leaving the normal races to divide the lands between them. The elves had vanished. Their histories, their culture, their songs, nothing had been left behind and Roanne had heard they had made mighty enchantments with their singing. Tobar and Kaylin knew tales of the elves that would make the mind spin with wonder. There were very few left who knew any tales of elves. Those that did insisted the elves had always been the defenders of the human lands and that someday they would come back to destroy the threat of the Trolls. Tobar had called them naive dimwits. No one else dared mention the accursed race. They were gone and the description of their race erased from the great libraries, save the king's. The king of that time had forbidden anything to be taken out of the great archives. Tobar did not believe the great archives held the truth anyway and he had laughed when she had expressed her wish to go there someday. Kaylin had not laughed. Roanne stumbled when her skirt was caught by a bush. Clutchng the vial tightly she let out a startled noise but she did not drop the vial. Carefully she pulled her skirt from the bush. Then they continued along the path. She could tell Tobar was at the end of his strength. Always before when she had stopped Tobar had stopped too but he kept going without a word. How much strength was left in that weathered old hide of his?

The path leveled out and widened. The hot springs bubbled up above, where Roanne had not gone. The stones set up in small walls and sections collected the warm water below. Moss covered most of it but by this light Roanne could not see the slimy green moss. Tobar spoke a glyph word. The sound of it made Roanne jerk up straight in her stance. Magic she recoginized. He let go of the sword. The sword hovered there above the stone wall of the first springs. The white cloth slid partially off its blade when the weapon began to tilt. Tobar spoke the word of power again adding his hands for emphasis. The sword righted itself in midair.

"The vial," he held out his hand.

Roanne set the vial into his hand, glad to be rid of it. Tobar moved to uncork it then halted. He looked back at Roanne and there were trenches of wrinkles driven into his brow.

"Go back," he told her.

"Back?" cried Roanne in surprise. "But..."

"Go back to the village," Tobar said firmly. "I don't want you ever coming up here again."

"But what if..."

"What if what?" Tobar grinned grimly. "What if I do not come back down. What if I build a shack near the hot springs and spend the rest of my days here? Would you be offended, would you deny me what little happiness I might have in life for the remainder of my days?"

"Tobar!" Roannne protested. "You are not that old!"

"Ask Kaylin," Tobar muttered. "She will tell you I have a right to my rest. Go home and if I don't come back go with Kaylin or stay and live with Brad and Hanna. They would treat you well."

"What is all this silliness about going back!" Roanne bit the bottom of her lip with a stubborness born out of necessity in dealing with Tobar everyday.

"I want you to be safe," Tobar sighed.

"Safe!" blurted Roanne. "And safe is carrying a vial of who knows what up a mountain path in the dark with a skirt on with nothing more than that little sphere of light to show us the path?

Tobar shook his head slowly. "We do what we must...the more you are around me the more dangerous the vials you would be carrying up mountains. Go home while you are still sane and if anyone ever comes asking around for me again tell them you are an orphan and you had no idea there was ever anyone named Tobar who existed!"

Roanne's eyebrows lifted in her delicate face. "We do what we must" was the beginning saying of the seven. Unable to waste anymore of his strength trying to convince her to leave Tobar turned to the sword. His hand freed the cork from the vial and he began to chant.

"We do what we must,
this will kill,
this will leave dying in the streets for centuries
to come,
but we do what we must.
Innocent blood will be shed,
but without this,
there would be nothing left,
and the bodies of all would be consumed.
We are guilty of a sin,
a greater sin than our fourfathers
but we do what we must
And we pray you

Let not the blood fall on our hands
Or the hands of our children."

Tobar spread the clear liquid upon the blade. The blade flared crimson searing the liquid away but Tobar's hand came up restraining the magic fire and forcing it to die back down within the blade. His other hand came up below the sword gathering the stray drips of liquid into his hand. The vial he had placed below his hand received the steady clear thick liquid from between his middle fingers. Roanne watched, fascinated when the clear liquid began to eat through the blade itself. The blade was a Seeker, she was certain. She had never seen one before but the histories told they were black blades and only the makers could destroy them. She stared at Tobar. He had been one of the seven or he was on of the greatest fools in all the land for even attempting to destroy this thing. This was one of the blades the six had wielded, the blades that had destroyed the Essenceater Ghosts. Why was Tobar trying to destroy it, especially had he been one of the seven to forge the blades? It made no sense.

Tobar's hand shook, his words faltered. Roanne leapt forward muttering words of strength under her breath. What woud happen should he go into a seizure now in the middle of this spell? Her right hand wrapped around his shoulder. She did not want to know. Tobar steadied himself and continued, not having the strength to give her the glare she deserved.

"Unmake the made
Untwist the twisted
Take the essence from within
And set the essence free."

Tobar's shaking legs collapsed beneath him. His limbs thrashed at the stone wall, the plants, the soil, and everything else within reach. The clear thick liquid ran into the vial, fleeing the sword without his aid. The crimson flames that Tobar had tamed flared within the sword's blade threatening to devour the vial and everything beneath it including Tobar. Roanne ran forward chanting a spell of shielding but it did not keep the flames away. Roanne reached for the sword's blade with her bare hand and screamed when the pain jolted through her body. She fell catching herself on the stone wall and the sword fell with her splashing into the depths of the hot spring pool below. Roanne tried to breathe but no air came out of her lungs. Slowly she sank from the wall unable to take in a single gasp of air no matter how hard she tried. Tobar caught her, his seizure had passed and he cursed himself for ever bringing her in the first place. His hands drew glowing blue circles of magic with her limp fingers. She must live and he needed the strength. He was growing old and weak, he should not have placed Roanne in danger, no matter the cost that would have to be paid later. Tobar cradled her to his chest. Then he looked into the pool below. The silver handle of the Seeker gleamed in the depths. Tobar squinted at it sending a wave of illusion to guard its position among the rocks. Muttering more words Tobar rose to his feet hoping his borrowed strength would be enough to bring Roanne home to Kaylin. Waving a hand at the vial he brought it with them floating eerily in the air behind, uncorked. This was pure foolishness but he could think of no other way to bring Roanne home.

There were a few steps more and then he came to a cleared space on the path where there were no trees blocking his view of the valley. Tobar saw the fire below and fell to his knees in despair. The bottle of uncorked liquid sank down behind him landing without ever spilling a drop of its lethal substance. Tobar's head sank. The war had begun again. There was nowhere to go except back up to the hot springs.

Far out on the road, with the fingertip of a moon overhead, Ev sat against the slight hill covered in grass and looked towards a much larger hill. His hands ran over the leather texture of the boots Kaylin had offered to him and he had taken without giving an offering in return. He grimaced. He had liked the boots but there was no Kaylin to give an offering in return to now. He stared out into the distance searching for a road or a larger hill. He had drifted into the plains for awhile following the river. He looked up above, picking out his favorite bright shines in the heavens. He was not lost. Based on what he saw he looked farther to his right. Ev Vrin was not lost but a Maekmorth would have been had he strayed so far from the group in strange territory. He did not remember when he had discovered this trick with the bright shines but by finding his favorite bunch of them above he could always determine in what direction North lay. He shook his head. Maekmorth did not have the time nor the interest to do this though he had tried showing his mother this trick. She had grunted and scolded him for thinking. Jhahgror had told him that his mother had scolded him for the reason that she thought so little of herself.

Jhahgror was the Troll who did not believe thinking was a bad thing. Ev looked away with that thought then pulling aside his leathers he stared at the small discoloration of his skin. The rock had hit there and, he pulled aside another section, the other had hit there. The coloring was fading rapidly. Ev looked again to the South and finally spotted the hill of Maekmorth.

Letting the leather fall back into place he rose from his sitting spot. The Maekmorth were horrible creatures, he had come to learn, but humans were no better, just weaker.

Grasses brushed against his shins when he walked through them in the direction of the hill of

Maekmorth. Lightning cracked above reminding him of the longer sword he carried. Reminding him of the knowledge that he was being watched by something he could not smell. He did not jump when the thunder rumbled behind him but his hand lingered over the hilt of Urr.

## Ch. 6 Ancient Magic

"Where is the sword?"

Roanne awoke near the wall of the lower hot springs hearing this voice and she could not believe her eyes when the ghostly elven form made its way up the path. Four dwarves accompanied it. Tobar jerked at the sound of the ghost's voice. The dwarves drew weapons.

"I know you are here Tobar, I can feel you!" the Essenceater Ghost stood beyond the wall of the lower hot springs.

Tobar stood slowly making a staying motion with his hand to Roanne. Roanne minded him and kept her head below the stones working her way around the walls until she was behind the wall of the higher springs. Tobar looked out over the wall of the springs. His hand closed over the vial that set upon the wall behind him. The dwarves moved around the wall of the lower springs.

"The sword Tobar, where is it?"

"I do not have it," Tobar answered.

"But you failed to destroy it," the voice said coldly.

"I will try again," Tobar's voice was steady.

"You will give the sword to me."

"I will destroy it, as we agreed," Tobar stated.

"Tobar," the voice chilled colder. "I have left your daughter alive. I have left you alive all these years to live in peace and what do you do in return. Instead of notifying me that you had found the last Seeker you tried destroying it yourself and failed! You will give the sword to me."

The dwarves were nearly past the walls of the lower springs. Tobar watched them but his focus was on the white figure in the middle. His fingers clenched tighter around the uncorked vial. Roanne stared up at the hatred in his face. Then she saw the blade of the first dwarf who was coming around the wall. Tobar cast the vial. Silver liquid spilled forth directed by the fingers held outspread above it. The silver liquid sprayed into the dwarves and the ghost. Roanne peeked above the wall for the second time when the terrible shrieks rattled through the air. The blades dropped. The dwarves had fallen to the ground, some rolling to rid their skins of the substance that was eating through their skin and even their boots. The white figure threw aside the veil the silver liquid was eating through, showing that she was not quite the ghost Roanne had feared. Her silver eyes narrowed and her lips moved to part. Tobar pulled himself over the wall of the higher springs and fell backwards into the hot waters below.

The sprinkles from the splash touched the skin of Roanne's face. She cried out and rose once his hand was gone from her trying to see what had happened. The woman in white stood there with her mouth wide. Wind struck the air bringing with it an evil charring smell that Roanne feared, but when it struck her she could not breath. Gasping for air that was not there she glanced back and saw no sign of Tobar beneath the clear waters of the spring. Then she fell forward into the waters of the hot springs. Beneath the surface the waters burned her skin, but she swirled her fingers in a small spell of cooling to keep herself from dying. She searched for Tobar but his body was not there.

Lower and lower her body dropped through the waters until her shoulder hit something hard and metal. Her hands reached around it clutching the handle of the sword. It came away easily from the slippery rocks. Staring at the blurry dark blade she wasted no more time, tucking it under her arm, she swam for the surface. Sputtering she broke through to the air. Her free arm wrapped around the top of the stone moss wall keeping herself from going under with her surprisingly light weapon. Evil laughter echoed in the air. Roanne paid it no mind pulling herself over the wall she fell through the air on the other side and rolled down the hill beneath it. Her body stopped before a pair of white slippers. Wiping the water from her eyes she stared up into narrow silver eyes.

"Give me the sword child!"

The small bit of air that Roanne's starved lungs had been able to bring in was sucked into that mouth along with far more but Roanne lifted the blade. The woman opened her hand to accept it. Roanne changed the angle and rammed it into the ghost's stomach. The essence of the ghost swirled into the blade. Ash drifted into the wind.

What little air remaining in Roanne's chest left her. Blackness covered her eyesight and evil winds howled around her safe refuge of darkness. There was a shrieking that pierced the eardrums and then silence. Roanne's body ached hellishly and her mouth was dry, her lips cracked, and the blood drained from her face. She took a breath and another when her lungs finally began lifting and falling. Shoving at the ground she managed to make it to her knees. Her eyelids scraped down in a blink that pained her. Water formed in them, slowly but when they came she found her head was less dizzy. The world stopped spinning and the dark splotches became light.

The dwarves were gone, eaten by the silver substance that fled back into the vial once its work was finished. All that remained were their blades. Tobar was gone. The evil woman was dead. She could not quite believe the woman had killed Tobar, her tears dripped onto the rocks. She rocked herself on her knees holding the black blade of the sword to her and trying to remember the few names of the seven that she had heard in Kaylin's stories. She was alone. The fresh wind that came from the mountains to the west blew strands of her hair across her pale face. Her hands curled around the black hilt of the sword weighted on the end with true silver. She bit the bottom of her lip. So this was the beginning of the adventure she had longed for all her life, and she could not keep the tears from sliding down her cheeks and falling to be lost among the dark grains of soil that dirtied the wet skirt covering her shivering knees. The sword's blade cut into her unprotected skin where her arm crossed it drawing blood into the blade causing it to glow with dark red fire.

## Ch. 7 The Maekmorth and The Ky

Ev sat around the fire with the rest of the Maekmorth listening to Crogar growl at him about the wasted offering of the head. Wolves had devoured it the night Ev left and it had fallen from the brittle tree branches. Ev privately suspected Mogrim, for she was deft at faking wolf tracks, but he said nothing.

Crogar went on to proclaim how he killed the Maekmorth chief Skur yesterday when the last clan of Trolls had come in to share in the raid to the human dwellings. He had killed Skut and now had a small clan of his own. Someday he would have a clan bigger than Grael's! They all chuckled over this knowing Ev was Grael's son and that any true son of Grael would have killed Crogar long ago, but that was what could be expected of a weakling misborn. Ev stared into the fire. It hurt his eyes but he stared into the fire. Why bother killing Crogar? What would he gain but a pack of idiots at his heels?

Mogrim's large lip sank low over her long bottom fangs. She was pouting. Mogrim had asked Ev to kill Crogar before. She hated the male and she would kill him herself but she was not as wily as Jhahgror. Mogrim preferred to keep her physical contact limited to other things. Ev had avoided her for a long time and Mogrim was more than certain she was the reason he had left a couple nights ago, but she could not figure out what she had done to make him leave. Ev would be a scrawny catch for her but he was the son of Grael and that alone made him worth the effort. The problem was that he did not behave in the same way the other Maekmorth behaved. Ev Vrin was a rule unto himself. When he decided to kill Crogar he would kill Crogar until then all she could do was wait and show her displeasure, the lip sank lower.

Qwor suddenly jumped from his log throwing curses into the air with his foul breath, running away from the fox crouched nearby. Qwor was terribly afraid of foxes for no reason the other Trolls could comprehend. He had once crawled into a fox's den with his brother when they had been a month out of the birthing cave. The memory of their needle sharp fangs would live forever in his small brain. Crogar snatched the fox up by the tail, being quicker than the average Troll.

"We cook it now," Crogar winked. "Then maybe Qwor fears no more foxes after he eats one."

Crogar thrust its struggling snapping form toward the fire. The fox melted into a clear substance reforming into a mountain lion. Any other Maekmorth might have let go but Crogar never let go of what he did not understand, he squeezed it tighter bringing in his other hand. The cat growled, screamed and dug its claws into his thick hide, filling its fangs with his dirty fur. Crogar grunted and thrust it into the fire, sure that whatever it was it would cook the same as any fox. The smell of scorched fur permeated the air. Ev looked up watching Qwor loudly proclaim the terrible attributes of all foxes.

"Frail One!" the human sounds screamed with the shift of the mountain lion into a shape that was more than recognizable.

Kaylin! Ev came to his feet. The shape melted back into a mountain lion scoring Crogar across the left cheek. Ev jumped forward thrusting the smallest blade he had into Crogar's side. The Troll grunted dropping the mountain lion into the fire. The shape melted and shifted into the only shape Kaylin knew of that could heal itself. Sparks flew on all sides. Croger's huge fist wafted air onto

Ev's nose when Ev dodged the blow but it was not until Ev reached for Kle that Crogar reached for his own blade. The wide blade was wickedly curved with spiked edges. Drawing the sword from the harness on his back the huge Troll raised it above his handsome head to divide this ugly misborn's skull in half.

Ev's fingers went right through the handle of Kle. His teeth grit in surprise and rage, but he had no time to investigate thin air. Straightening to the side of Crogar he let Crogar's blade sweep past his chest. Drawing Urr he cut into the Crogar's throat splattering blood everywhere. Mogrim licked the drops that had fallen on her thick skin. Crogar's great mass fell backwards with the swing of the blow, half beheaded. Ev let go the handle of Urr dodging an attack from behind. He barely heard the noise but the impact of the huge mace glanced past his shoulder leaving a crushing blow behind it. Ev's shoulder went numb and he could not move the fingers in his right hand but he drew the smaller blade from his belt with his left and placed his foot on the head of the mace that was driven into the dirt by force of the muscle behind it.

Qwor snarled trying to lift the weapon faster than Ev could run up the handle and ram the small blade under his chin. The Maekmorth's eyes went empty with that last thought. Ev rode the corpse down on its long fall backwards onto the earth. His silver eyes raised. Mogrim was pleased, she was grinning from her nostrils to her pointed ears, but the newer Trolls were not. They looked on him uneasily as their new leader, and they wanted him to provide their next meal. Maekmorth after Maekmorth stood waiting to hear what he had to say. The pain in his shoulder was excruciating but Ev did not let it show. He brought the tip of his smaller blade up pointing towards the north.

"Sheep," he told them. "Slow fat sheep, thirty rock throws of Ogar. Who wants to lead the raiding party?"

The Maekmorth turned their black eyes over the Golden Plains straining to see this new meal promised them. Several Maekmorth grunted including Mogrim. Ev chose the closest and barked an order for them to move. They could not see the sheep but he could, and ever so slowly they began heading in the direction he had pointed. Mogrim went following their leader, for no female Troll would be beat out of the first meal provided by their new chief. Ev breathed trying not to let the dancing dots in front of his eyes take over his vision. He stepped off the giant corpse and fell to his knees misjudging the distance. He crawled forward taking the hilt of Urr and pulling it from what had been Crogar. He heard a noise and crawled over to investigate. Kaylin was there but not as he had seen her. She was more vivid, taller than the short human woman. Her hair was redder and her eyes were slender. She opened them slowly. Half her face was burnt though it was healing rapidly in between the two sharp tipped ears.

"Ev?"

Ev slid up beside her lowering the blade of Urr over her throat. Her eyes went wide. Ev studied the healing burn scars on her skin having seen similar burn marks heal before this on his own flesh.

"What race are you," Ev snarled.

Kaylin shifted beneath the edge of the blade but he held it to her. The stone he wore around his neck sparked against his chest and the shift ended in the same form it had began. Her eyes darkened. Her body stilled.

"Ky. You wear a runestone and yet you do not know my race?"

"That sound means nothing to me!" Ev's snarl was violent, the blade pressed against her throat.

"A Shapeshifter!" Kaylin clarified.

The blade remained close enough to scratch her. Ev considered this. Shapeshifter...the meaning was in the human sounds and what his own eyes had witnessed.

"Is that what I am?"

"No," Kaylin answered him. "Shapeshifters are shapeless beings of energy that may still themselves into matter. We have no form. We borrow our shapes from others. We are what we make ourselves."

"And I am not?"

"You are not," Kaylin agreed.

"But you are me?" Ev stared down at her with a great look of confusion written on his sharp features. "One of me?"

The pupils of Kaylin's eyes moved down towards the blade. Ev removed it. The burns on her face were nearly healed.

"Yes," she replied sitting up cautiously. "I am shifted into one of your race."

Ev kept Urr near her body. Its tip pressed to her side to make her understand he would not allow her to leave. Animals he could track but she had already proven she could shift into more than one and how would he find the right one?

"What are my race?"

"Elves," Kaylin replied rubbing the back of her sore neck, Ev pressed the blade closer to her hide.

"Where are my race?" his silver eyes were intense, Kaylin looked away.

"I do not know, the elves vanished long ago," Kaylin replied. "I do not know where they went."

"Who does?"

"No one," Kaylin could not keep her eyes from that silver stare. "I don't know if you can find them, Ev. Even if you could search for many, many years."

"But I am not Ky?"

"No, you are not Ky and the Ky do not know where elves went," Kaylin said softly touching the blade with her thumb and redirecting it carefully away from her body. "I must go now."

"Go...why?" Ev did not allow the blade to be redirected.

"I must warn king Jotham about the Maekmorth," Kaylin replied. "It is what I came here to do."

The blade pressed into her clothing, "You warn the king. He sends an army against Maekmorth."

Kaylin nodded slowly. "We will fight for our land."

"Maekmorth land!" Ev's growl was low.

"Elven land," Kaylin replied setting a hand to his shoulder. "Your land."

Ev's growl did not cease. Kaylin's words were in there, but he did not know how to respond. Among the Maekmorth it was easy. Kill or let live. He could do this here. Forget all the other complex things in his head and decide in simple terms to kill or not to kill, but he found when he took away the headache threading its way into his brain the answer was simple and already made. He lifted the blade away. Kaylin touched the stone beneath the leather on his chest. What was the sound she used for it? Runestone, he remembered.

"Keep this," she whispered. "No one else must take this. Do you understand?"

Ev nodded slowly. He wanted to ask what it was and why she thought it important but his tongue had dried to the roof of his mouth. Kaylin stood, lifted her arms to the north, and her shape rippled. The cry of a hawk split the air. Kaylin took to wing. Ev watched her fly through the sky to the north. Grass waved beneath her wings. The wind touched his face but Ev ignored it. He watched the hawk until it was no longer a black dot in his keen vision. Then crouched and wiped the blood from Urr's blade. He had a race. He was not a misborn the way his Maekmorth mother always told him, and he would find that race. He was not Maekmorth. He rose from his crouch sheathing Urr. Wind rippled through his fair hair and his silver eyes squinted south, towards the Scartooth Mountains.

www.ingramcontent.com/pod-product-compliance
Lightning Source LLC
LaVergne TN
LVHW050941080826
845145LV00004B/1362

* 9 7 8 0 6 1 5 2 4 5 0 0 3 *